I PICKED HIM
A Nick and Emerson Story

Thomas J. Torrington

First Printing: 2019

ISBN- 9781099210211

Nick and Emerson

www.nickandemerson.com

Published by Thomas J. Torrington

torrington@protonmail.com

www.thomasjtorrington.com

My name is Emerson.

I am a puppy.

When I was very little, my brothers, sisters, and I were neglected.

Nobody was there to love us.

I got very sick.

We were saved and brought to a rescue shelter in Maine.

A rescue shelter is a place that
takes care of lost and
lonely animals.

At the shelter, I got better.
But now, I was deaf.
Deaf means I couldn't hear anything.

I watched as boys and girls came and adopted all of my brothers and sisters.

Happy boys.

Happy girls.

Happy dogs.

But not me.

I didn't understand why
no one picked me.

Was it because I couldn't hear them say, "Good boy?" or, "sit," "lie down," or "speak?"

I was sad.

one day, a boy named Nick
came to the shelter.

He didn't seem to react when the other animals made noise.

He was deaf.

Just like me.

I didn't want to wait
to be picked anymore.

So, I picked him.

And Nick took me home!

He knew how to speak without words.

And he taught me to listen without hearing.

I learned when to sit.

I learned when to lie down.

And I learned when to speak.

Best of all, we both
learned to say, "I love you"
without any words at all.

Now, Nick's a
happy boy.

And I'm a happy dog.

A happy dog.

Glossary
(words we learned)

neglected: not taken care of

rescue shelter: a place that saves animals and finds them forever homes

deaf: not able to hear well, or at all

adopted: taken to a new forever home

react: act like you notice something that happens near you

Made in the USA
Monee, IL
18 February 2020